Oozey Octopus

HAPPY READING!

This book is especially for:

Crase, Benjamin on Sarah

Suzanne Tate,
Author—
brings fun and
facts to us in her
Nature Series.

James Melvin,
Illustrator—
brings joyous life
to Suzanne Tate's
characters.

Suzanne and James in costume

Oozey Octopus

A Tale of a Clever Critter

Suzanne Tate
Illustrated by James Melvin

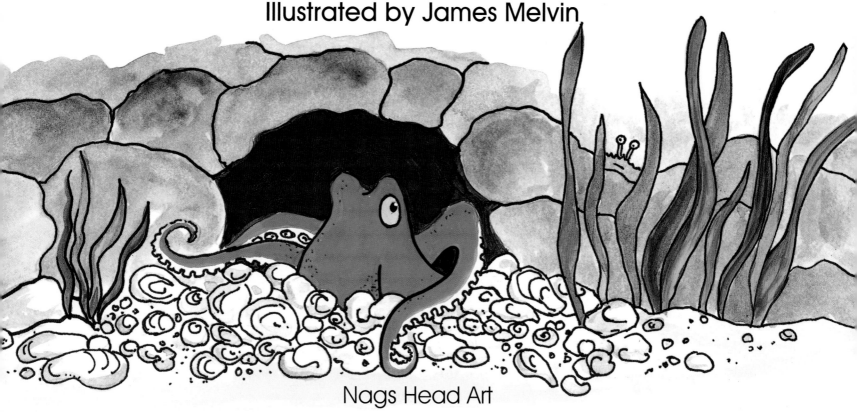

Nags Head Art
Number 22 of Suzanne Tate's Nature Series

To Grandma Ruth
who was always
there for us

Library of Congress Catalog Card Number 99-96240
ISBN 978-1-878405-26-5
ISBN 1-878405-26-8
Published by
Nags Head Art, Inc., P.O. Box 2149, Manteo, NC 27954
Copyright © 2000 by Nags Head Art, Inc.

Oozey Octopus was a strange-looking critter
with long, squirmy arms.
He was a member of the mollusk family
with its hard-shelled oysters and clams.

But Oozey had no shell to protect him.

Underneath his head was a beak like a bird.
And he had big eyes and a large brain.

Oozey Octopus was much smarter
than any oyster or clam!

He had eight powerful arms.
Each one had two rows of suction cups
that helped him fight or catch food.

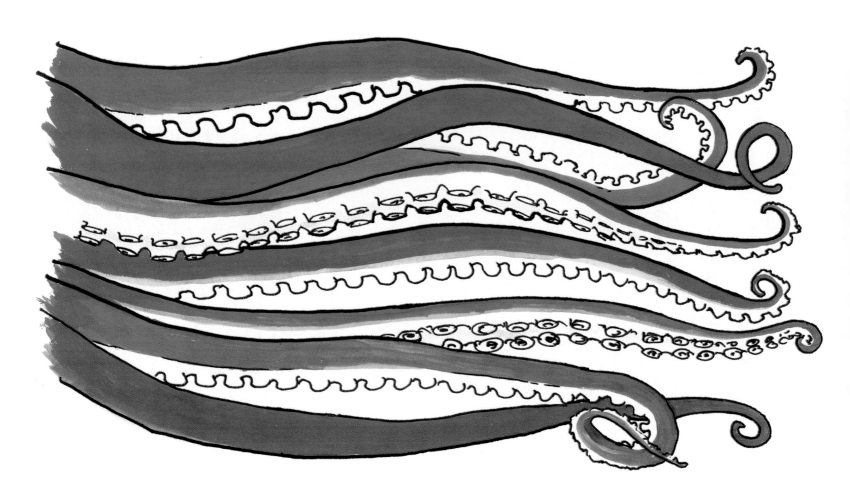

Oozey Octopus lived all alone.
His home was a den where
he could hide from enemies.

He was a messy mollusk!
Many old shells littered the opening
to his den.

At dusk, Oozey would slip out of his den.
He would ooze in and around everywhere,
looking for food.

Oozey Octopus liked to hunt for crabs —
a favorite food.
First, he squirted a cloud of ink into the water.
It would help him hide.

Then he oozed along the bottom and began
to sneak up on crab after crab.
He caught each one with a squirmy arm.

Crabby and Nabby were nearby!
"Look, there's that big octopus we've
seen before," Crabby said.
"Yes, and look at all those poor crabs
he's caught," Nabby sighed.

"Quick, let's bury in the bottom," Crabby urged.
Crabby and Nabby hid just in time.
Oozey Octopus oozed right over the top of them!

When Oozey arrived home with his harvest
of crabs, he slipped backwards into his den.
"I'll be safer this way," he thought.
"I can watch to see if anything

is out there!"

The next day, Oozey peeked out of his den
with his big eyes.
Carefully, he oozed out and about.

Oozey Octopus was always careful
because he had many enemies.

Suddenly, a big stargazer was near!
Oozey tried to hide by instantly changing color.
But that hungry fish came closer and closer.

Oozey let go a powerful weapon — an inky cloud that usually stopped anything.
But that big fish kept coming. He opened his mouth and in went Oozey!

Oozey Octopus was in big trouble — but not for long!
The stargazer couldn't swallow Oozey
with his squirmy arms and big head.
That ugly fish spit him out — arms and all!

Oozey shot a jet of water through his body
and sped away!
"Oh my," thought Oozey, "what a close call.
I'm going to look for a new place to hide."

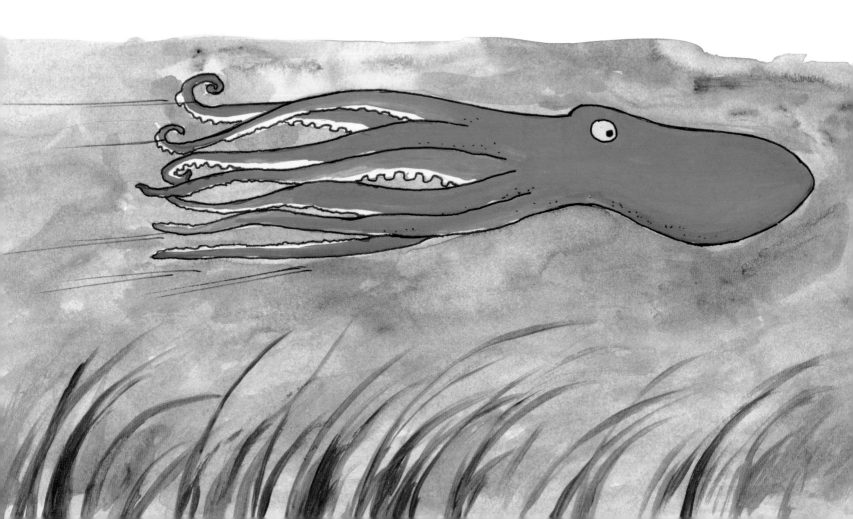

Then he saw that one of his arms was missing. But Oozey wasn't worried — he knew that it would grow back!

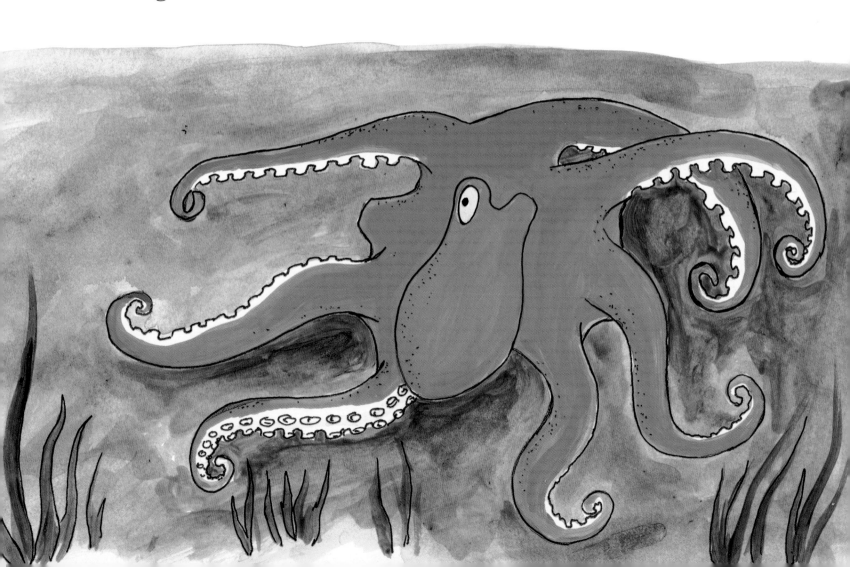

The big octopus found another hiding place
and went to sleep.
When he woke up, Oozey sensed
something scary!

Some strange animals were swimming in the water
near his new den.
Oozey oozed out a bit so that
he could see better.

"I've never seen anything like those creatures before," he thought. "They look like dolphins that would like to eat me. I'd better stay in my den where I am safe."

Oozey Octopus oozed into his den again.
Shy and smug, he lay hidden from the world.

And like every other octopus —
Oozey was always a clever critter!

The HELPFUL HUMANS saw right away
how clever an octopus could be.

"It didn't take long for him to get that shrimp,"
one of the divers said.
"Now we see how quickly an octopus
can solve a problem."

But in a few minutes, Oozey's big brain told him
just what to do.
He turned the jar lid with a squirmy arm
and grabbed a shrimpy treat with another!

Oozey was excited to see the shrimp.
He oozed out to grab a tasty treat,
but it was inside the jar!
"What kind of trick is this?" he asked himself.

The HELPFUL HUMANS wanted to find out
just how clever an octopus could be.
They swam away where Oozey
couldn't see them.

Oozey Octopus didn't know that
those strange animals were divers.
HELPFUL HUMANS had come to study him.

They placed a glass jar with a lid near Oozey's den.
In the jar, there was a juicy shrimp
— a tempting meal for an octopus!